ISLAND HERITAGE™
PUBLISHING
A DIVISION OF THE MADDEN CORPORATION

94-411 Kō'aki Street, Waipahu, Hawai'i 96797-2806
Orders: (800) 468-2800
Information: (808) 564-8800
Fax: (808) 564-8877
islandheritage.com

ISBN NO. 1-59700-492-8
First Edition, Fourth Printing - 2012
COP121804

The Story of ALOHA BEAR

Written by **Dick Adair** • Illustrated by **Stephanie Britt**

ISLAND HERITAGE™
PUBLISHING

There was a stowaway
on Santa's sleigh
the night he left the pole.

2

A furry little bear
in underwear,
a warmer place his goal.

He hid among the toys
for the girls and boys
who lived out in the sun.

He went undiscovered
'til uncovered
when Santa's work was done.

4

6

"What do I see
under that tree?
Did I put that there?

Where on my list
did I put this
fuzzy yellow bear?"

7

8

"Your eight reindeer
helped bring me here,
though no one really knew.

I snuck my way
aboard your sleigh
and then hid from your view.

I used to get so lost
in all that frost –
the cold, cold snow and ice.

The nights so long,
the wind so strong.
It really wasn't nice.

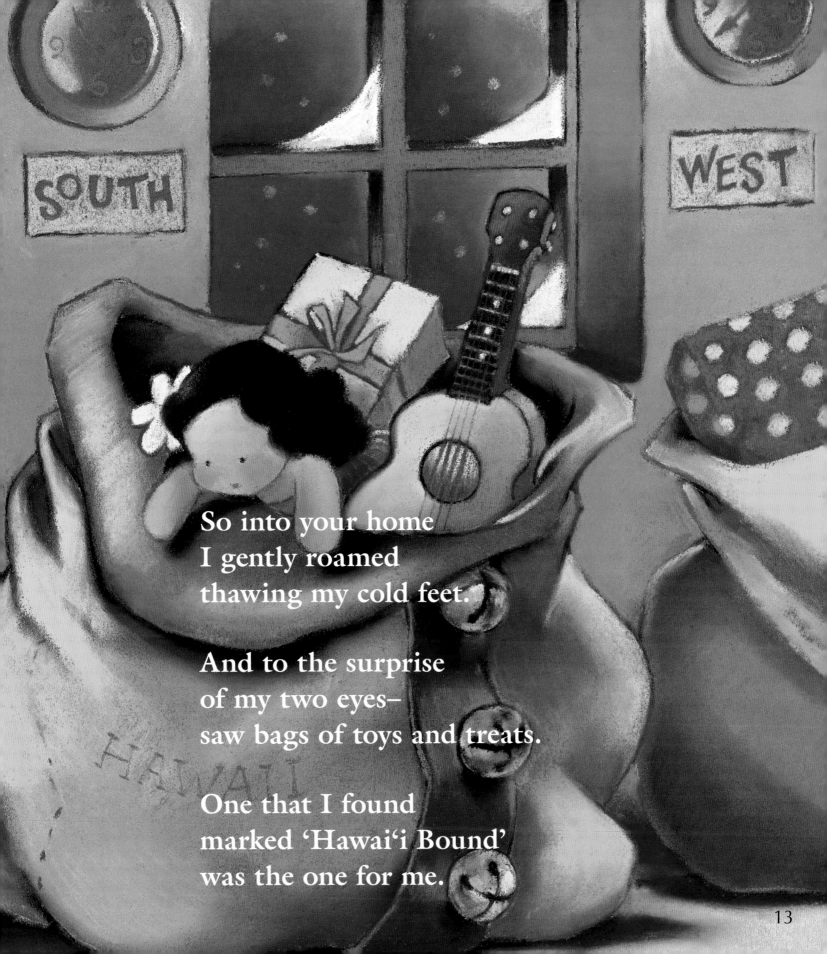

So into your home
I gently roamed
thawing my cold feet.

And to the surprise
of my two eyes—
saw bags of toys and treats.

One that I found
marked 'Hawai'i Bound'
was the one for me.

13

So I jumped inside
to await my ride
to an island out at sea,

where trade winds blow
and days are slow.
I just had to see

where the grass skirts shake
and the big waves break.
It's paradise to me.

And what was in store
was warm surf and shore.
My trip, I couldn't delay.

As I could not face
that icy, cold place
Oh Santa, please let me stay!"

With a twinkling smile,
Santa thought for a while,
about the events of the night.

It was a welcome pause
for ol' Santa Claus
after his long flight.

He looked around
that's when he found
no gifts on his sleigh.

For Hawai'i was his last stop,
his favorite spot,
where palm trees always sway.

Now this small bear
with soft, golden hair
would be in for a treat.

For
Santa

18

"Do not be sad.
You should be glad.
People here are sweet.

I'll now leave you
to this fine beach view.
Until we meet again.

20

With a grateful smile
in this beautiful isle,
this creature had lots to share.

He escaped the cold.
Now his story is told.
And now he's

ALOHA BEAR.